P9-CDZ-348

REVIEW COPY

What's Looking at You, Kid?

By **J. Patrick Lewis**  Illustrated by **Renée Graef**

For Beth, Matt, and Leigh Ann

—Love, Dad

This book is dedicated to Holly and David.

—Renée

Waves can make
the ocean roar.

Waves can scrape the ocean floor.

Look who's walking on the shore.

Have you ever
touched a star?
This one
wasn't
very
far.

Look who's in a jelly jar.

To sip a flower,
then dive
and dart,

Her wings
beat like her
little heart.

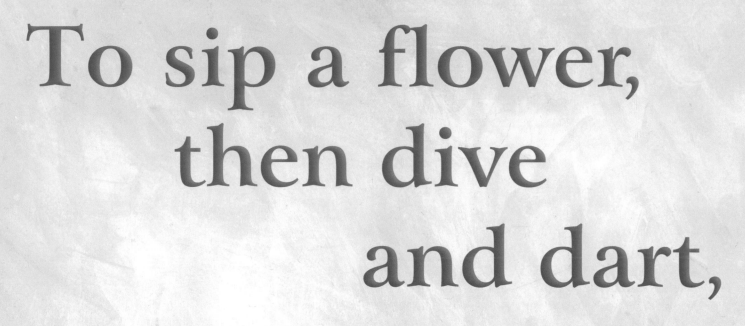

Look who likes to
stop
and
start.

Look who's
sleeping
in the
sun.

She is
lots of
dots of
fun.

See if you can count each one.

Oh, it
must be
very hard

when a robin's
standing
guard.

Look who's
hiding in
the yard.

Up and down,
high and low,

Surprises everywhere you go.

Look who's tickling your toe.

Look who's into something sweet.

She must live on
Honey Street.

Buzz
Buzz

She's got honey on her feet!

Hanging in the air's the thing he can do without a wing.

Look, a yo-yo on a string!

Whee!

Skimming ponds and country lanes,

whizzing wings
of windowpanes.

Look, a pair
of fairy planes.

In the barn
under the hay,
that's the
warmest place
to play.

Look before she runs away!

She just loves
to tease the cat,

who is coming
up to bat.

Look at what he's
swinging at!

A truck carries
a heavy load.

A car does not like being towed.

Look who else can cross the road.

Or is that a rainbow spray-on?

Look at how her colors stay on.

My favorite
animal indeed
is one who always
loves to read.

Look at those eyes.
Can you guess who
they're looking at?
It must be

YOU!

Text Copyright © 2012 J. Patrick Lewis
Illustration Copyright © 2012 Renée Graef

All rights reserved. No part of this book may be reproduced in any manner
without the express written consent of the publisher, except in the case of brief
excerpts in critical reviews and articles. All inquiries should be addressed to:

Sleeping Bear Press™
315 E. Eisenhower Parkway, Suite 200
Ann Arbor, MI 48108
www.sleepingbearpress.com

Sleeping Bear Press is an imprint of Gale, a part of Cengage Learning.

Printed and bound in the United States.

10 9 8 7 6 5 4 3 2 1

Lewis, J. Patrick.
What's looking at you, kid? / J. Patrick Lewis ; [illustrated by] Renée Graef.
p. cm.
Summary: Simple rhymes and illustrations are used to help explore
and identify wildlife such as birds, insects, and sea creatures.
ISBN 978-1-58536-793-1
[1. Stories in rhyme. 2. Animals—Fiction.] I. Graef, Renée, ill.
II. Title. III. Title: What is looking at you, kid?
PZ8.3.L5855Wh 2012
[E]—dc23   2011032088